A NOTE TO PARENTS

Early Step into Reading Books are designed for preschoolers and kindergartners who are just getting ready to read. The words are easy, the type is big, and the stories are packed with rhyme, rhythm, and repetition.

We suggest that you read this book to your child the first few times, pointing to each word as you go. Soon your child will start saying the words with you. And before long, he or she will try to read the story alone. Don't be surprised if your child uses the pictures to figure out the text—that's what they're there for! The important thing is to develop your child's confidence—and to show your child that reading is fun.

When your child is ready to move on, try the rest of the steps in our Step into Reading series. **Step 1 Books** (preschool–grade 1) feature the same easy-to-read type as the Early Step into Reading Books, but with more words per page. **Step 2 Books** (grades 1–3) are both longer and slightly more difficult, while **Step 3 Books** (grades 2–3) introduce readers to paragraphs and fully developed plot lines. **Step 4 Books** (grades 2–4) offer exciting nonfiction for the increasingly independent reader.

The grade levels assigned to the five steps are intended only as guides. Some children move through all five steps very rapidly; others climb the steps over a period of several years. Either way, these books will help your child "step into reading" in style!

www.randomhouse.com/kids/

Library of Congress Cataloging-in-Publication Data
Herman, Gail. The lion and the mouse / by Gail Herman ; illustrated by Lisa McCue.
    p.   cm. — (Early Step into reading)   SUMMARY: An adventuresome mouse proves that even small creatures are capable of great deeds when he rescues the King of the Jungle.
ISBN 0-679-88674-5 (pbk.) — ISBN 0-679-98674-X (lib. bdg.)   [1. Fables.   2. Folklore.]
I. McCue, Lisa, ill.   II. Title.   III. Series.   PZ8.2.H43Li 1998 398.24'529757—dc21[E] 97-38601

Printed in the United States of America   10 9 8 7 6 5 4 3 2 1

EARLY STEP INTO READING is a trademark of Random House, Inc.

The Lion and the Mouse

By Gail Herman
Illustrated by Lisa McCue

Random House 🏠 New York

PART 1

Little Mouse.

Big Lion.

Big, big trouble!

"Let me go!"

begs Mouse.

"Someday

I will help you!"

10

"YOU help ME?"
says Lion.
"Ha, ha, ha!"

But Lion opens his paw.

He sets Mouse free.

PART 2

Big Lion.

Big net.

Big, big trouble!

ROAR!

Mouse sits up.

He follows that roar.

"Help me!"
begs Lion.

Mouse starts to chew.

He chews

and chews.

He sets Lion free!

Lion does not laugh
at Mouse now.
Now he knows...

...even the
littlest Mouse
can help
the biggest Lion.